Tilly the Terrier

Written and Illustrated

By Ben Simons

Tilly the Terrier

By Ben Simons
© 2016 Ben Simons

9780993526572

First published in 2016 by Arkbound Ltd (Publishers)
Written and Illustrated by Ben Simons

Arkbound is a social enterprise that aims to promote social inclusion, community development and artistic talent. It sponsors publications by disadvantaged authors and covers issues that engage wider social concerns.

Arkbound fully embraces sustainability and environmental protection. It endeavours to use material that is renewable, recyclable or sourced from sustainable forest.

Arkbound
Backfields House
Upper York Street
Bristol BS2 8QJ
England

www.arkbound.com

Tilly the Terrier

Ben Simons

Published by Arkbound

I am charming and delightful
I wonder why life is this easy

I hear my name shouted in frustration
I see free food,
that's too much temptation

I want attention when I'm not myself
I am charming and delightful

I pretend I'm upset to get
My wishes fulfilled

I feel sorry for all the teddies
I've killed

I worry you won't come back

I wag my tail from side to side

Every time the car pulls up on the drive

I am charming and delightful

I understand I can't pee inside

I say let me out

With my bark as my shout

I run towards any cat that I see,
I just want to play
But it's not meant to be

I cry for a ball and a big open field
I am charming and delightful

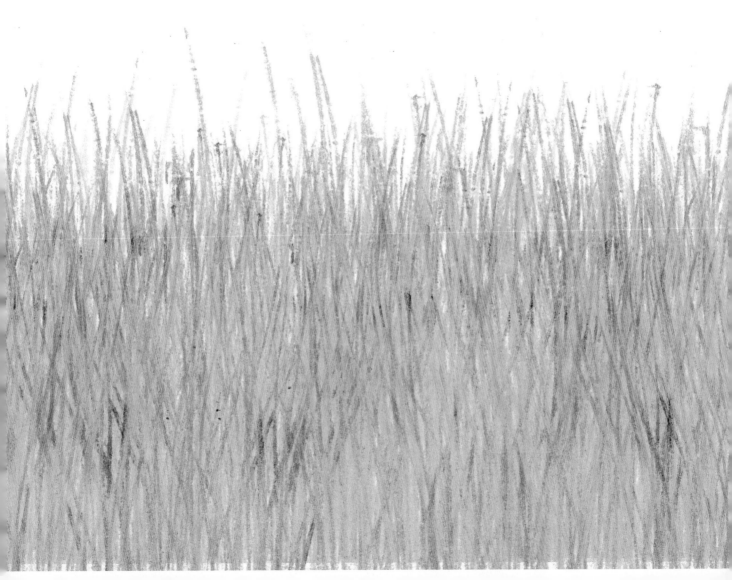

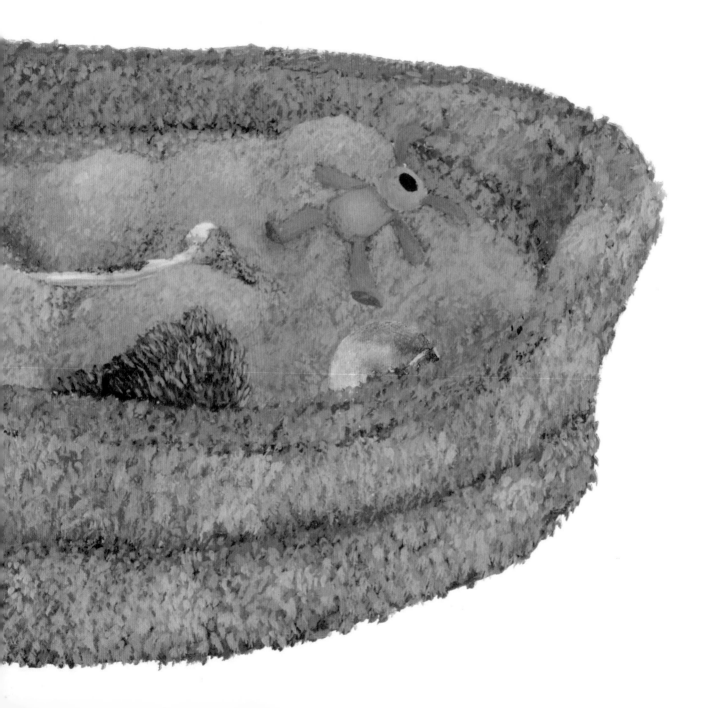

My favourite thing, after I've been fed
Is to chew on my bone and lay on my bed

I dream there are more hours to sleep
I try not to snore
But my breathing's too deep

I hope you love life as much as I do
I am charming and delightful

About Tilly

This book is based on a small Border Terrier from Bristol named Tilly. She is a very loving and caring dog who is easy going but still enjoys going on long walks and chasing her ball.

About Ben Simons

Ben is a 20-year-old illustration student studying at University for the Creative Arts in Farnham, Surrey. He has a strong interest in illustrating childrens' books and designing fiction book covers.

This is Ben's first book to be published and he is very excited to start creating more. If you would like to contact Ben please use the email below. To see some more of his work take a look at his website and Instagram.

bensimons.illustrator@yahoo.co.uk

www.bensimonsillustrator.wix.com/website

Instagram - @bensimons.illustration

Printed in Great Britain
by Amazon